BOOK 1: THE CURSE OF THE BOLOGNA SANDWICH

In which superhero Melvin Beederman and third-grader Candace Brinkwater team up to stop bad guys in Los Angeles.

BOOK 2: THE REVENGE OF THE McNASTY BROTHERS

In which the McNasty Brothers escape from prison to get revenge on Melvin and his partner in uncrime, Candace.

BOOK 3: THE GRATEFUL FRED

In which Melvin and Candace must find who is out to get rock star Fred of The Grateful Fred.

BOOK 4: TERROR IN TIGHTS

In which a mysterious e-mailing enemy nearly dooms Melvin and Candace, those partners in uncrime.

Coming Soon:

BOOK 5: THE FAKE CAPE CAPER

In which Melvin heads to Las Vegas for the Superhero Convention, leaving Candace in charge of Los Angeles.

MELVIN BEEDERMAN SUPERHERO

TERROR IN TIGHTS

GREG TRINE

ILLUSTRATED BY
RHODE MONTIJO

HENRY HOLT AND COMPANY ★ NEW YORK

For my brother Mike
—G. T.

For my brother Abel
—R. M.

Henry Holt and Company, LLC
Publishers since 1866
175 Fifth Avenue, New York, New York 10010
www.henryholtchildrensbooks.com

Henry Holt® is a registered trademark of Henry Holt and Company, LLC.
Text copyright © 2007 by Greg Trine
Illustrations copyright © 2007 by Rhode Montijo
All rights reserved. Distributed in Canada by H. B. Fenn and Company Ltd.

Library of Congress Cataloging-in-Publication Data
Trine, Greg.
Terror in Tights / Greg Trine; art by Rhode Montijo.—1st ed.
p.   cm. — (Melvin Beederman, superhero)
Summary: When Los Angeles superhero Melvin Beederman starts receiving
mysterious, threatening e-mails, he and Candace, his partner in uncrime,
must figure out who is out to get him and then do something about it.
ISBN-13: 978-0-8050-7923-4 / ISBN-10: 0-8050-7923-8 (hardcover)
1   3   5   7   9   10   8   6   4   2

ISBN-13: 978-0-8050-7924-1 / ISBN-10: 0-8050-7924-6 (paperback)
1   3   5   7   9   10   8   6   4   2

[1. Heroes—Fiction. 2. Los Angeles (Calif.)—Fiction. 3. Humorous stories.]
I. Montijo, Rhode, ill. II. Title.
PZ7.T7356Do 2007   [Fic]—dc22   2006017718

First Edition—2007
Hand-lettering by David Gatti
Book designed by Laurent Linn
Printed in the United States of America on acid-free paper. ∞

CONTENTS

A HIGH-TECH THREAT

Superhero Melvin Beederman was just minding his own business, doing what he did second-best. What he did best, of course, was save the world, chase down bad guys, and make the city of Los Angeles a better place to live. But he wasn't doing that. He was doing his second-best activity—hanging out in his tree house hideout, eating pretzels with his pet rat Hugo, and watching his favorite TV show, *The Adventures of*

Thunderman. Thunderman and his assistant Thunder Thighs also saved the world. In every single episode. Watching them always inspired Melvin to do his job a little better.

When the show was over, Melvin decided to check his e-mail before starting his day. "I think I'll go save the world," he said to Hugo.

"Squeak," Hugo said in reply.

This either meant "You do that, kind sir," or maybe "Do you want to have a push-up contest?" Melvin was never sure what Hugo was saying. Though he had once been fluent in gerbil, talking to a rat was another story.

He turned on his computer and found only one e-mail waiting for him. But it was a doozy.

I'm coming to get you, Melvin Beederman. Don't try hiding. I know all your tricks and your weaknesses. And when I find you, you'll be toast! Smashed-beneath-my-feet toast.

Your loving enemy,
SC

P.S. Consider yourself doomed!

SC? Melvin didn't know any SC. He caught bad guys for a living, so there were plenty of people who wanted revenge. But who was SC? Melvin thought over some of his recent battles. Joe the Bad Guy? No, wrong initials. The McNasty Brothers? Nope, couldn't be.

Melvin looked at the return address imgoingtogetyou@ifitsthelastthingido.pew for a clue.

"Holy mystery!" Melvin said out loud. "This ain't good."

Holy mystery, indeed! It wasn't (narrators never say "ain't").

There was only one thing to do, Melvin decided. He had to talk it over with his partner in uncrime, Candace Brinkwater. He always felt better talking to Candace. Unlike Melvin, who was an orphan and had graduated from the Superhero Academy, Candace lived in a normal house with her family. She was not from the academy. She was just a girl with whom Melvin had divided his cape. As they say, two superheroes are better than one. And Los Angeles was happy to have both of them.

"See you later, Hugo," Melvin said as he moved to the door of the tree house.

"Squeak," Hugo replied, which either meant "Go get 'em, tiger!" or "How do you spell kumquat?"

Melvin wasn't sure. And right now he was too distracted to think about it. Someone was out to get him, and he had to find out who.

"Up, up, and away," he said as he jumped out the door.

Crash! He hit the ground hard.

That was the thing about Melvin Beederman. He hardly ever got off the ground in one try.

He brushed himself off and tried again. "Up, up, and away."

Splat!

And again. *Thud!*

Once more. *Kabonk!*

On the fifth try he was up and flying. He flew over the city toward Candace Brinkwater's house. As he flew, he looked down at the people of Los Angeles. Melvin didn't know how to turn off his x-ray vision, so instead of seeing people dressed for work, he saw them in

their underwear. Hundreds of them. Thousands. Disgusting, he said to himself. Too disgusting for words. It was even too disgusting for punctuation!

! * ?) . ; , , " ' ! ? # % ! (! & @ : ?

See? That didn't help at all.

THE PARTNER IN UNCRIME COMES
UNDONE—AND UNGLUED

While Melvin was busy having his life threatened by whoever was at imgoingtogetyou@ifitsthelastthingido.pew, Candace Brinkwater was having problems of her own.

What were they, you ask? Well, for one thing she had a math test coming up, and math was her worst subject. For another thing, there were at least seven former bullies at her school who were now forced to be good because they had a superhero keeping them in line—and they didn't like it at all. But these were small problems in Candace's eyes. There was something much bigger.

Smedley was dead. Candace's beloved dog Smedley, who she sometimes called Smed for short, was dead. "Holy pet cemetery!" she said. "This is bad news."

Holy pet cemetery, indeed! It was.

With Smedley gone to that big dog-house in the sky, Candace didn't feel like doing anything. She didn't clean her room. She didn't do her homework. She didn't even do her nightly one-arm push-ups—500 each arm. She just sat around and moped.

"Maybe you can get another dog," her mother suggested.

Candace, of course, didn't want another dog. Smedley was a hard act to follow, especially when he was chasing his tail. He'd always been there for her, when she was struggling with math or when she came home after a long day of saving the world with her partner in uncrime, Melvin Beederman.

The morning after Smedley had died, Candace was still in mope mode.

"Hurry, Candace, you'll be late for school," her mother said.

Candace did as her mother told her. But she didn't fly to school that morning like she usually did. She was too upset for that. She walked instead. It was the first time she'd walked since becoming a superhero, and it felt strange. She thought back to how she'd come across Melvin Beederman's cape after a mix-up at the dry cleaners, and how lucky she was that he'd decided to divide the cape with her. They had been partners in uncrime ever since.

Only now she didn't feel like being a partner in anything. And she was certainly in no mood to save the world.

The other kids at school were surprised to see Candace walking to class. Wasn't this the girl who had run the hundred-yard dash in three and a half seconds? Hadn't she scored 500 points in a single basketball game? She was the only third-grader who could fly, for goodness' sakes! And here she was walking. Just walking.

The school bullies were the first to notice that Candace was not herself. Usually they had to behave themselves when she was around, but today she seemed distracted.

"Now's our chance," Johnny Fink said to his best friend, Knucklehead Wilson. It was first recess, and Johnny and Knucklehead were standing under the goalposts, their usual spot. "Go punch a second-grader, Knucklehead, and report back to me."

"Candace Brinkwater is right there. She'll see me."

"She's different today," Johnny said. "Trust me."

"You sure?" Knucklehead hated that a girl could get the best of him—and a third-grader at that. But when he looked over at Candace, he saw what Johnny was talking about. She was walking on the soccer field with her head down. Maybe he could punch someone and get away with it. It had been so long—he wondered if he remembered how.

He went over to a second-grader, checked to see if Candace was watching, then punched the kid. It all came back to him. "Just like riding a bike," he said to himself. He punched the kid once more. It was nice to be a bully again, he thought. He had missed the old days.

The second-grader squealed in pain, of course. But Candace did nothing.

"See that?" Johnny said. "She doesn't care. Gather all the other bullies, Knucklehead. We're back in business!"

HOLY BAD POETRY!

Melvin flew across town toward Candace Brinkwater's house. Below him things were bustling as the whole city of Los Angeles came to life. Cars of every size and shape. People, too, for that matter. And underwear.

"Ugh! Did you have to mention the underwear?"

Sorry, Melvin.

He was almost too distracted to

notice the underwear. Almost. Once again, someone was out to get our superhero. And as Melvin flew, he kept remembering the bad guys he'd caught recently. Every one of them had reason to hate him, but none had the initials SC. None that he could think of anyway. Maybe it was Santa Claus. That was the only SC who came to mind. But no, he had been a good boy that year. Besides, he hadn't gotten coal in his stocking. That was usually the first clue that Santa was peeved. If you got coal, you were in trouble.

Melvin flew on and on, pausing only once to flex at his reflection in the windows of the tall buildings. Usually, he took his time with flexing, but today he had too much on his mind.

"Who is SC?" he said out loud.

Maybe Candace would have an idea. She was pretty terrible when it came to math, but she did have good ideas. "Gotta get to her before school," Melvin said to himself.

On most days, Melvin didn't see Candace until after school, when they met at the library. This was so Melvin could help her with math. He tutored her in math and she helped him save the world. It was the perfect arrangement. It was only because of the threat that Melvin had decided to go to her house.

He never made it.

Suddenly a police siren screamed. Melvin glanced down and saw what looked like a chase. Bad guy—good guy. And Melvin was on the good-guy side.

Talking to Candace would have to wait.
Melvin raced to help.

"Stop the car!" he told the driver as he
swooped down on him.

When the driver didn't stop, Melvin stopped the car for him. Then he dumped the bad guys onto the street as the police pulled up.

"Nice to have a superhero in town," said one of the police officers.

"Just doing my job," said Melvin. This was part of the Superhero's Code. And Melvin always kept to the code.

He waited around until the bad guys were handcuffed and stuffed in the back of the patrol car, then he took off again.

At least he tried to.

"Up, up, and away."

Crash!

Splat!

Thud!

Kabonk!

Up and flying again on the fifth try. By the time Melvin reached Candace's house, she was already in class. He would have to wait until after school to talk with her. And so he patrolled the skies and waited. . . .

That afternoon he got to the library early and checked his e-mail on one of the computers.

Roses are red,
Violets are blue,
I'm going to get you,
If it's the last thing I do.

SC

Another threat from whoever was at imgoingtogetyou@ifitsthelastthingido.pew.

"Holy bad poetry!" Melvin said. Everyone in the library shushed him, including the librarian—green underwear and all.

Holy bad poetry, indeed! Melvin had no idea who it was or how the person knew his e-mail address. Hopefully, Candace Brinkwater would help him find the answer.

IFITSTHELASTTHINGIDO.PEW

SC stands for Superhero Carl, of course. Only he was no longer a superhero. He'd had his cape taken from him because of his unsuperhero-like behavior. Ever since then, he'd spent his days thinking up devious and sinister ways to get back at Melvin Beederman. Sometimes devious, sometimes sinister—it was all the same to Carl. Just as long as Melvin suffered.

He used the initials SC to confuse Melvin Beederman. Maybe he'd suspect Santa Claus. When Carl had had his cape taken from him for creating the unofficial Melvin Beederman Web site, which blabbed Melvin's weakness around the world, he'd found himself stranded in Fiji. He was all alone, with no super powers to help him get back to America. He washed dishes at one of the hotels to make some money. And soon he was heading back to get his revenge.

Carl was now a bad guy, as bad as they come. He even used words like nincompoop when addressing his own captain! Still, there was a part of him that missed his superhero days (even if they were unsuperhero-like).

He missed stopping trains, outrunning speeding bullets, and bench-pressing Buicks. Most of all, he missed the respect.

Here on the *Good Ship Lollipop*, where he signed on as a dishwasher, he was treated like dirt by the other crew members.

"Hey, shorty, there's a spot on my glass."

"Hey, shorty, clean this plate and make it snappy."

"Hey, shorty, you're short!"

He was. But what did they expect from a nine-year-old? Life was not much fun for the former Superhero Carl. And the worse his life became, the more he blamed his troubles on Melvin Beederman.

"You'll pay for this, Melvin," Carl grumbled, "if it's the last thing I do."

It was horrible to be a bad guy on a ship called *Lollipop*. He had wanted to cross the ocean on the *Bad Ship Lemon Drop*, but they already had a dishwasher. *Lollipop* . . . the name alone made it hard to be devious, let alone sinister.

Carl worked long hours in the kitchen. Then he dragged himself to his room, which was in the belly of the ship. His only joy was the few minutes each day when he could send nasty e-mails to Melvin Beederman. He'd get his revenge. He was sure of it. But there was one thing he had to do to make it happen. He needed a cape, a real super-hero's cape. And he knew just where to get one: the Superhero Academy.

He would steal one of the retired capes from the academy, along with a set of tights. He hated the thought of wear-ing someone else's tights, but if they gave him the strength to choke the life out of his least-favorite superhero, then it was worth it. Carl lay on his

bunk thinking about it. He smiled as he imagined Melvin's doom. Then he began to sing.

Doom dooby doom doom doom.
Melvin you are doomed.
Dooby doom doom doom.
Melvin you are doomed.
Wah, wah, wah, wah-ah.

A bad guy with a song in his heart? What's wrong with this picture?

CANDACE AND MELVIN
PUT THEIR HEADS TOGETHER

Melvin noticed that something was not right the moment Candace walked into the library for their afternoon math session. "What's the matter?" he asked her.

She tossed her backpack onto the table next to Melvin. "Smed is dead."

"Poor Smedley," Melvin said. "I loved that little guy. He was the best tail chaser I've ever seen."

"Exactly. And he could howl at the moon like nobody's business."

Melvin wasn't so sure about that. His own father used to howl at the moon all the time. Sometimes he'd do duets with a local Doberman pinscher.

"Sorry to hear about Smedley," he told his partner in uncrime.

"Thanks." Candace grabbed her math book from her bag and flipped it open. "We'd better get started with my homework. Would it be okay if we didn't save the world today? I'm a little down."

What? Not save the world? Had Candace Brinkwater lost her marbles?

"Not save the world?" Melvin said. "Have you lost your marbles?"

Candace gave Melvin a look. "I thought we weren't going to repeat what the narrator says."

"Oh, sorry. Are you nuts? We have to save the world. It's what we do. There are cries for help every day in this town, and we have to live up to the Superhero's Code."

The code was something Melvin had learned at the Superhero Academy. You can never say no to a cry for help, according to the code. The problem was Candace had not graduated from the academy. She didn't know the code, and she didn't care.

"I don't know the code, Melvin, and I don't care."

"I thought we weren't going to repeat what the narrator says."

"Oh, sorry. Code, shmode. Better?"

"Much," Melvin said.

But not that much. Candace still didn't want to save the world!

Melvin decided to change the subject. "Someone's out to get me, Candace."

"What else is new?" Candace said. "It's part of the job, don't you think? You put bad guys in jail and they want revenge."

He told her about the e-mails. "Do the initials SC mean anything to you?"

"Hmm . . . maybe. Did you get a lump of coal in your stocking last Christmas?"

"I've already thought of that. It's not Santa Claus. He's not the smash-beneath-his-feet type."

"Man, that would hurt—a fat guy like that stepping on you."

Melvin gave her a hard look. "It's not Santa. Trust me. Who else do we know with those initials?"

Candace thought this over, then shook her head. "I'm clueless."

So was Melvin.

They finished Candace's homework, and then launched themselves outside the library. Well, at least Candace did. Melvin joined her in the air a little later, after . . . uh . . . you know.

"Don't say a word," Melvin told Candace as they zoomed across the sky.

"Did I say anything?" Candace replied. "Sheesh, some superheroes. Let's go save the world, Melvin."

She didn't feel like saving the world,

but someone was out to get her partner in uncrime. He needed her help.

As they flew, Melvin couldn't stop thinking about who was out to get him. Who was SC?

MEANWHILE . . .

While Melvin and Candace were putting their heads together and trying to solve the mystery, Carl and the *Good Ship Lollipop* were sailing closer to America.

"I can't wait to get started on my devious and sinister plan," he said. It was too early to decide if his plan would be devious or sinister. He just knew Melvin would be in pain very soon, and the thought made him smile.

Carl had finished washing the dinner dishes and was now in his quarters with his laptop computer. "One more e-mail ought to do it," he said to himself. "That'll let him know I mean business."

And Carl did mean business. He had hated Melvin ever since his days at the Superhero Academy. But that hate had grown over the last few months. With every dish he washed and with every disrespectful comment from the crew, Carl thought of his former classmate Melvin and how to get back at him.

He could hardly wait to get to

America. The sooner he got there, the sooner he could steal a cape and tights on his way to Los Angeles.

$$\wedge\wedge$$

A few days later, the *Good Ship Lollipop* cruised into Boston Harbor at night, which, of course, was perfect for Carl. He couldn't very well steal a superhero's cape in the daytime. And he sure didn't want anyone to see that he had been on a ship with a name like *Lollipop*. Word could get around, and Carl had his bad-guy reputation to think about.

He left the ship as soon as it docked and made his way along the dark streets of Boston toward the academy. Once on the grounds, he moved silently, keeping to the shadows. He knew some of the student superheroes had very good hearing. They could hear a twig snap from a mile away. They could also see your underwear.

Several times Carl stopped to listen. All was quiet.

The Great Hall of Superheroes was on the first floor of the academy. This was where the retired capes were displayed. And there were many, from all the great superheroes who had come and gone before Carl. Superhero Charlie, Superhero Fremont, Thunderball, Mega Biceps. . . . Their capes and tights were hung on the walls as a tribute. Carl didn't care which set he took, just as long as he could get some powers back.

He picked the lock on the door and

crept inside. Then he pulled a small penlight from his pocket and shone it on the wall. "Grab the first set and get out of here," he said to himself.

He did. He grabbed and ran. Outside, he put on the cape and tights and launched himself. "Up, up, and away!" Carl was up and flying on the first try. He streaked across the sky, heading for Los Angeles.

With any luck he'd be there by morning.

Then he could set about getting revenge on Melvin Beederman—squashed - beneath - his - feet Melvin Beederman.

HUGO'S ADVICE

Melvin got another e-mail from the same location, another threat signed by SC. But then the e-mails stopped. Maybe it was all a joke, he told himself. And so he went back to saving the world. After all, catching bad guys was what Melvin did best.

He caught bank robbers and car thieves, drug dealers and all-around devious dudes. And sinister ones. This helped keep his mind off SC. Well, sort of. It was in the evenings, when Melvin was back at his tree house and things were quiet, that the thoughts returned. He turned to his pet rat for advice. Candace wasn't around after dinner, so Hugo would have to do.

Melvin looked at the rat, who was eating pretzels and flipping the channels on the TV, looking for an *Adventures of Thunderman* rerun.

"What do you think, Hugo, should I be worried about those e-mails? They seem to have stopped."

Hugo looked at him. "Squeak squeakity."

This might have meant "I recommend being prepared at all times, you handsome guy in a cape, you."

Or maybe it was "I'm considering taking up racquetball."

Melvin thought this was good advice, at least the part about being prepared. If Hugo wanted to take up racquetball, that would be okay, too. Melvin would keep his guard up at all times, in either case. And maybe he should watch Thunderman and Thunder Thighs for pointers. They always came out on top.

"Pass the pretzels, Hugo."

Hugo did. Once again, Thunderman and Thunder Thighs saved the world. And they did it in under thirty minutes, including commercials. They even had time for a preview of next week's episode. Melvin turned off the TV, ignoring Hugo's squeaking protests.

The Adventures of Thunderman wasn't real life, he told himself. Even though the threatening e-mails had stopped,

Melvin felt strange, like some invisible thing was coming for him. What it was, he couldn't say. Sure, he caught bad guys for a living and all of them hated him for it, but they didn't have e-mail in prison, did they?

He went to the window and looked down at the lights of Los Angeles, and the strange feeling continued. Was SC real? Was he or she or it still out to get him? Melvin didn't know. He turned to his rat roommate. "Keep an ear peeled, Hugo. We may have a visitor."

"Squeak squeakity squeak squeak squeaken squeaker." This was a very long sentence for a rat. It either meant "Will do, good buddy who needs to give me the TV remote" or "Who do you like, the Dodgers or the Red Sox?" You could never be sure with rat talk. At least Melvin couldn't.

"Just stay alert, Hugo."

Melvin moved a chair to the window so he could stay alert also. Hours went by. He didn't sleep a wink. Finally, he decided to do a little nighttime saving of the world. Usually he hung out with Hugo after the sun went down, eating tasty snacks, watching TV, and telling knock-knock jokes. This night was different. He had to get out and do something to keep his mind off his worries.

He launched himself in his usual way—crashing, splatting, thudding, kabonking—flying on the fifth try, and went on patrol. He broke up a bar fight on Melrose Avenue. He stopped a run-away bus on Wilshire. He caught a few

kids spraying graffiti here and there. Then he danced the night away at Fast Eddy's Amazing Disco and All-Night Car Wash.

It was a very busy night for Melvin Beederman. Still, it wasn't enough. He couldn't stop worrying about who was out to get him.

LIQUID BOLOGNA?

Carl was really zooming. Boy, had he missed it! It had been a long time since he'd had the full powers of a superhero. And now, as he sped across the sky, heading to Los Angeles and Melvin Beederman, he decided to use those powers doing the things he loved. *It'll bring back those fond memories of my days at the academy,* he thought. Besides, he needed to brush up on his skills.

And so he stopped a speeding train just to see if he still could. No problem. "Just like riding a bicycle," he said to himself. Then he bench-pressed a Buick. This wasn't easy, because the Buick was racing down the road when he grabbed it and bench-pressed it. But he managed. He was as strong as ever, he decided, and raced on.

Could he see through walls? He stopped in front of a building to try it out. Yes, his x-ray vision was perfect. He even got a glimpse of someone's underwear. Unlike Melvin Beederman, Carl could turn his x-ray vision off and on at will, which made it much less annoying. Seeing everybody's underwear all the time had to be a pain in the Melvin.

This was how Carl thought of his enemy. Melvin had achieved rear-end status.

Carl kept flying, heading for the West Coast, and practicing all his old moves—steep dives, quick turns, stopping on a dime. Or a quarter, since that

was all he had. He'd been out of practice for a long time, while Melvin saved the world on a daily basis. Carl had to be ready to face him. And so he kept at it, zooming, zigging, zagging, bench-pressing, Melvin-hating.

Then suddenly he stopped, midair. He'd thought of something. Bologna was Melvin Beederman's weakness. He couldn't show up in Los Angeles without it. Somewhere in Utah he found an all-night grocery store and stocked up. Bologna by the slice. Bologna by the slab. Fried in a sandwich. Bologna by the log. Bologna from the hog—hey, that rhymes! Sliced, diced—you name it, he bought it. He even thought he might invent something called liquid bologna and spray it all over Melvin. Just thinking about it made him excited.

"Look out, Melvin Beederman. Here I come," he said.

The sun was just rising as he launched himself again outside the grocery store. He'd be in Los Angeles in no time. The question was, could he find Melvin once he got there?

Fortunately, Carl had graduated from the academy, too. He thought like Melvin in some ways, because they were trained at the same school. He knew the code. "Where would I make my hide-out?" he asked himself as he raced across the sky. "Where would I set up my superhero headquarters if I were Melvin Beederman?"

THINGS GET BACK TO NORMAL . . .
OR DO THEY?

Hugo's advice was sound, Melvin decided, even though he wasn't exactly sure what that advice was. If it was "Keep up your guard at all times," then it was good advice. And Melvin decided to follow it.

He went back to his normal routine of catching bad guys, but he did it cautiously, always noting everyone's initials as he went. So far, no one with

SC turned up except Santa Claus. And he wasn't exactly a devious dude. Fat and jolly, yes; out to get Melvin, not likely. As Melvin had said, you know when Santa is peeved by what he leaves in your stocking.

Melvin met Candace at the library after school, as usual.

"What's the latest?" she asked him. "Any more news from SC?"

Melvin shook his head. "The e-mails stopped, but I'm keeping an eye out. How are you doing? How's life without Smedley?"

Candace shrugged. "I still miss him, but maybe I'll feel better if I catch a few bad guys. Do you think I can bust through a couple of locked doors while I'm at it?" This was the superhero perk that Candace loved the best. Catching bad guys was okay, but busting down doors—now that was fun!

"Sure. I'll even lock them myself," Melvin said.

"You're so good to me."

The two superheroes worked some math problems together, then launched themselves outside the library.

Or at least Candace did. She always got off the ground on the first try.

Not Melvin. "Up, up, and away."

Crash!

Splat!

On the fifth try, Melvin joined his partner in uncrime in the air. Candace looked at him and smiled. "You're the worst flying superhero I know."

"Don't rub it in," Melvin said as they

streaked across the sky. "Let's go catch a bad guy or two."

"And kick in some doors," Candace added. "Don't forget the doors."

"I won't." Melvin hovered in front of a tall building with shiny windows and flexed.

Then they flew on and on, looking for bad guys. Little did they know that the worst bad guy of all was already in town.

INFLATABLE LAIR?

The problem was, Carl couldn't find Melvin. All day long he searched. Los Angeles was too big, too spread out. There were too many people.

"Holy needle in a haystack!" he said. "This isn't going to be easy."

Holy needle in a haystack, indeed! It wasn't.

And so, at the end of the day, with no sign of Melvin Beederman, Carl decided he'd need a place to stay while he came up with a plan. Where did a bad guy go to find a place to live?

You guessed it. Big Al's Rent-a-Lair. Not hideout—lair. As everyone knows, Big Al has been serving Southern California's bad guys since 1985, and that was good enough for Carl.

"What have you got in your economy line?" Carl asked Big Al. He was saving his money in case he had to buy more bologna.

"Are you sure you don't want to check out our lair with a built-in Jacuzzi? It's very popular among bad guys your age."

"I'm on a budget," Carl said. "In fact, do you have any portable lairs?" He knew that bad guys had to be as mobile as possible.

"I have just the thing." Big Al walked over to a strange-looking lair in his showroom. "Our newest model. An inflatable lair. Light weight, economical, and holds up to police bullets quite well, believe it or not."

"I'll take it."

"By the way," Big Al said, "did you know you smell like bologna?"

Carl ignored this comment. As long as the bologna did its job, he didn't care what he smelled like. He bought the inflatable lair and set it up on the hill below the Hollywood sign. This was a very popular location for bad-guy lairs.

With his portable home all set, Carl made a bologna pizza and went out on the front porch to eat. From there he had a great view of the city. It was the perfect place to plot Melvin Beederman's doom.

Now Carl just had to find him. Where was that superhero with flying problems? How should he track down the world's-worst train stopper? The guy with the funny hairdo . . . the keeper of the code—

Carl nearly choked on his pizza. "Of course!" he cried. "The Superhero's Code!" Melvin always followed the code. And what was the first rule of the code? Never say no to a cry for help. If Carl put someone in danger, Melvin would have to come to the rescue.

Carl knew this was the answer. He also knew that bologna pizza was the worst thing he'd ever tasted.

THE TRAP

Melvin kept checking his e-mail. There was nothing more from SC, but he couldn't stop thinking about it. Besides, he'd been trained at the Superhero Academy to sense danger. He sensed it, all right. Something nasty was afoot, which is a whole lot different than having something nasty on your foot. Or under it.

Melvin kept his guard up while he continued to save the world. And there was plenty to keep him busy. He spent his mornings catching bad guys on his own. In the afternoon, he teamed up with Candace Brinkwater after doing a little math.

Ah . . . math. It was the next best thing to catching bad guys or snacking on pretzels and drinking root beer.

But as the days passed and things got back to normal, Melvin forgot about his rat Hugo's good advice. It was Hugo who had first suggested that Melvin be prepared at all times. At least this is what Melvin thought he had squeaked. The point is, Melvin dropped his guard. And the more time went on, the lower it dropped. He was a sitting duck for anyone who knew his weakness.

Candace Brinkwater, on the other

hand, was still curious about the e-mails and brought it up every day at the library.

"Steve Coffin?" she said. "Stephanie Crookshank? Sammy Crouton?"

Melvin gave her a look. "What are you talking about?"

"The initials, SC. Aren't you curious who hates you? I am. I think about it all the time."

"That's probably why your math grade is slipping," Melvin said. He pointed to her textbook. "Finish these problems, and let's go save the world or something."

"And kick in doors?"

"If you like."

Candace smiled at the thought. It simply didn't get much better than kicking in doors. With Melvin's help, she finished the last of her math.

"Okay, let's g—"

And that's when they heard it. A cry for help. Someone was in trouble and the Superhero's Code told them what to do. Well, it told Melvin. Candace was clueless when it came to the code. But that didn't matter. She acted on instinct. Someone was in trouble and that's all she needed to know.

"Help!" The cry came again.

Our two superheroes ran outside and launched themselves, Candace on the first try. She hovered above the trees, waiting for Melvin to join her. "Let's go, Melvin! I see smoke."

"Be with you in a moment," Melvin said. "Up, up, and away."

Crash!

On the fifth try he joined her in the air. Candace pointed toward downtown, where smoke was rising. By this time, sirens were screaming, but there was another scream that only their super-hero ears could pick up—a human scream. "Help!"

Melvin and Candace streaked across the sky to the rescue.

THE FAKE DAMSEL

Carl didn't know what a damsel in distress sounded like. Not exactly anyway. But he had watched television over the years and he figured he could fake it.

He had started the fire on the tenth floor of what looked like an abandoned building downtown, then to put the finishing touch on his devious plan (or maybe it was a sinister one), he stuck his head out the window and screamed like a damsel.

It was this fake damsel cry that reached the ears of our two partners in uncrime.

Carl put his head out the window and yelled again in his high-pitched girlie voice. "Help! Somebody help!"

The streets below were busy with police setting up roadblocks around the building and fire trucks starting to arrive. Carl stood at the window with his binoculars, watching the sky for Melvin Beederman. He was ready with a good supply of bologna. Once the bologna took effect, Melvin would be at his mercy.

"I can't wait," he said to himself. Yes, getting his hands on Melvin Beederman—that was something he'd dreamed about for a very long time.

"Help! Somebody help!"

"A damsel," Melvin said as they zoomed across the sky.

"What?" Candace asked.

"It's a damsel in distress."

"Maybe it's just a guy with a very high voice."

Melvin nodded. "Good point." He didn't feel like arguing, but he was pretty sure he knew a damsel when he heard one.

Up ahead, they saw flames shooting out of a building, then another cry came. "Help!"

Melvin and Candace did just that. They broke through the wall on the tenth floor of the burning building, since flames prevented them from using the window. What they saw stopped them cold. In the middle of the smoke-filled room stood a boy in a cape.

"Ha! See? Not a damsel," Candace said.

"Not a damsel, indeed!" said the boy in the cape. "Hello, Melvin Beederman."

It was Carl, of course. The former superhero himself. He stepped to the side and pointed to a pile of bologna— by the slice, by the slab, fried in a sandwich, bologna from the log, bologna from the hog. Hey, that still rhymes! Sliced. Diced. He hadn't invented the liquid bologna yet, but it was on his to-do list.

Melvin and Candace began to feel weak. "Can't . . . move . . . get—"

And right then the floor gave way beneath them. Melvin and Candace fell through, leaving Carl and the bologna above.

"Holy lucky break!" said Melvin as he regained his strength. "Let's get out of here."

Holy lucky break, indeed! Getting out of there was a good idea. Staying away from the bologna was a very good idea.

Melvin punched a hole in the floor and he and Candace jumped through to the next level. Then he did it again . . . and again. They were several floors down when Candace realized what was happening.

"Wait a minute, Melvin. Let me do that."

"Do what?"

"Punch through the floor." After all, it was a lot like kicking in a locked door.

And so she did . . . *punch, punch, punch.* Before long, they were on the ground floor, racing to get away from Carl, who was screaming from above, "Curses! Melvin Beederman, I'm going to get you. And your little pal, too."

Then Carl grabbed his sacks of bologna and jumped through the hole in the floor and came after them.

Once they were out on the street, Candace turned to Melvin. "What now?"

"For starters we keep our distance from Carl. If he gets close with that bologna, we're history."

"Right."

They ran and ran.

"I thought Carl was decaped," Candace said as they raced through the streets.

"He was. Must have gotten another cape someplace."

"The academy?"

"Most likely."

They stopped in an alley to catch their breath. Melvin peeked around the corner to see where Carl was.

"What do you see?" Candace asked.

"He's coming." Melvin looked around for a place to hide. The alley was a dead end. There was no place to run, and Carl would be on them any minute.

"And the plan is?" Candace asked.

That's when Melvin saw it—a manhole cover. "In there," he said, shoving Candace ahead of him. He lifted the cover and jumped in after her, then slid the cover in place again. With any luck, Carl would pass on by.

"With any luck, Carl—"

"I know," Candace said. "Don't repeat

what the narrator says. It's annoying."

Above them they heard footsteps. Melvin looked at Candace and put a finger to his lips. They stayed motionless, eyes on the manhole cover. If it moved, they'd run; if it didn't they'd—

It moved! Light shone through the hole and there was Carl. "Hello, Melvin Beederman."

"Run!" Melvin yelled.

CANDACE BRINKWATER GOES AWOL

They did. They ran and ran though the dark sewer tunnels beneath the city. "Holy I-need-a-clothespin," Candace said. "It smells terrible down here."

Holy she-needs-a-clothespin, indeed! It did smell terrible. Then again, they were in a sewer. What did she expect, the scent of freshly baked muffins?

Candace and Melvin ran on, making as many turns as they could to throw

Carl off the trail. But with his extra-sensitive superhero hearing, it didn't work. Or maybe it was because he'd been trained at the same academy as Melvin and knew all his moves and his way of thinking.

In any case, our two partners in uncrime couldn't shake him.

"We can't shake him," said Candace.

"See? Now you're doing it," Melvin said.

"Sorry."

The sewer tunnels were dark, almost too dark to see, but they raced on anyway. What else could they do? If Carl got too close with the bologna, it would be curtains for Melvin and Candace. On they ran, until—

"Holy dead end!" Melvin said.

Holy dead end, indeed! They'd come to the end of a tunnel, it seemed. There were no side tunnels to escape through and they could hear Carl coming up fast. He'd be on them any second. Things didn't look good for our partners in uncrime. They were history.

"What is he saying?" Candace said.

"Who?"

"The narrator. There's gotta be a way out of this."

Nope. Sorry, Candace—you are history.

"We'll see about that!" Candace said.

"See about what, Candace? Where are you going?" Melvin asked.

Candace pointed up. "Out there. If he can't narrate properly, I will."

"Out there?" Melvin couldn't believe what he was hearing. "Outside the book? Candace, you can't! It simply isn't done."

"Oh yeah? You watch me." And with that, Candace was gone.

83

"Holy vanishing sidekick," Melvin said.

Holy vanishing sidekick, inde—

Hey, Melvin.

"Yes? Who's there?"

It's Candace. I've got things under control now. The narrator's . . . uh . . . tied up at the moment.

"What have you done, Candace?"

Never mind. Look above you. There's a manhole cover.

"Where'd that come from?"

I told you. I've got things under control. Go out through the manhole and I'll meet you.

"Candace, I can't get off the ground

in one try. And there's not enough room down here to get a running start."

Oh, right. I forgot. Look down, then. There's a trapdoor.

"How'd that get there?"

I wrote it right in there, baby.

"Oh. Well, thanks. Now get back in here, Candace. I'm going to need your help."

OOPS! CANDACE
FORGETS SOMETHING

"Wow, Candace, you're back already? That was quick. How did you know you could do that—go outside the book, I mean?"

"We had to do something. Carl was coming up fast—with bologna!"

"What's it like out there?"

"Just like here, only everything's in color."

"What's color?"

"It's hard to explain, but it's really cool."

"What's that supposed to mean?"

"I don't know how to put it, Melvin."

"Try. I'm curious."

"Okay, let's see. It's like eating your favorite ice cream with your eyeballs."

"I thought you said color was cool!"

"That is cool. Doesn't that sound cool?"

"No. It sounds downright freezing. Sorry I asked, Candace."

"You're sorry. How do you think I feel?"

"Uh-oh."

"What's the matter?"

"I just thought of something."

"What?"

"There's no narrative. Did you forget to untie the narrator?"

"Shoot! I think I did. What happens if we leave him tied up?"

"It means we're stuck in this tunnel forever, talking, and the story stops dead. You'd better go untie him."

"Okay, be back in a flash."

"Did you untie him?"

"Yeah. Why do you ask?"

"Because we're still stuck in this tunnel. No action, no speaker tags, nothing but this dumb dialogue."

"Hey, speak for yourself. I'm pretty good at this."

"Who cares? We're still stuck down here."

"Hey, as long as Carl's not around, we're okay."

"Maybe you should say something to the narrator, Candace."

"Why don't you talk to him?"

"Because I'm not the one who tied him up. Hey, wait a minute—where'd you get the rope?"

"I'll tell you later. Hey, narrator, are you there?"

I'm here.

"What gives? Can we get on with the story now?"

I'm waiting for an apology.

"Okay, it'll never happen again."

It better not!

WHO IS MEGA BICEPS?

And so our two superheroes ran down the new tunnel beyond the trapdoor created by Candace Brinkwater's narration. This tunnel was not a dead end, and they soon found themselves out on the street again.

Melvin stopped. "We need to split up," he said.

"What are you saying?"

"Carl is after me, not you. If we split

up, he'll follow me. He has a cape from the academy, which means he has a weakness. Get to a phone and call Headmaster Spinner. Ask him which cape is missing. If we can find out Carl's weakness, we can fight back."

And so Melvin headed off one way and Candace the other. "How will I find you again?" Candace asked as she was leaving.

"Listen for a superhero choking. It will be me. Carl has a deadly choke hold."

Candace raced home to use the phone. "Operator, give me the Superhero Academy in Boston."

"I'm sorry," said the operator, "there is no number for a Superhero Academy.

Are you sure you don't want Hero's Shoe Repair? Or possibly Super Duper Ice Cream Parlor? Or—"

"Never mind." Candace hung up. She'd have to fly to Boston. It was the only way to save Melvin. She ran outside and launched herself. She didn't bother saying "Up, up, and away." No time for that.

It had taken Melvin six hours to fly from the academy to Los Angeles, but he was sitting on the wing of a jet. Candace would have to make better time. Much better time. She flew so fast that her cape nearly tore in the wind.

She stopped only once. This was just outside Saint Louis, where she helped some firemen kick in a door. "Got

anything else that needs kicking in?" she asked them.

"No, but thank you."

Had she known the code, she would have said "Just doing my job, sir." But, of course, she had not graduated from the academy. She didn't know the code. She flew on.

When she arrived at the Superhero Academy, she went straight to Headmaster Spinner's office. "Melvin Beederman's in trouble," she said. She told him about Carl and the stolen cape.

"Holy unthinkable thievery!" said the headmaster.

Holy unthinkable thievery, indeed! They went to the Great Hall of Superheroes to check things out. Sure enough, there was a cape missing.

"He's got Mega Biceps's cape," Headmaster Spinner said.

"Great. What was Mega Biceps's weakness?"

The headmaster folded his arms across his oversized stomach. "Let's see. Ping-Pong balls? No, that's Superhero James. Jelly donuts? Hmm. Nope, that's Superhero Margaret." He scratched his chin and thought. "I got it! Kryptonite. That's it."

"That's Superman's weakness," Candace said.

"Oh, right." The headmaster thought some more. Then he smiled. "Got it! Mega Biceps's weakness is country music. Do you have any country CDs?"

"My dad does," Candace said as she rushed outside to launch herself. She just hoped she wasn't too late.

MEANWHILE . . .

While Candace was in Boston learning of Mega Biceps's (and Carl's) weakness, Melvin was running through the streets of Los Angeles, trying to keep out of range of the bologna. Melvin was as fast as a speeding bullet, it was true. But so was Carl.

This made it almost impossible to escape. Almost. Melvin had one advantage. He knew the streets of Los Angeles.

Carl didn't. After several twists and turns, Melvin lost his enemy.

He made his way back to his tree house. He was pretty sure Carl didn't know where he lived. The unsuperhero may have tracked down his e-mail, but no one knew Melvin's address. Trees don't have addresses.

Hugo was taking a nap when Melvin arrived. He opened an eye and gave a sleepy "Squeak?" This either meant "You look tired, big guy." Or maybe it was "Have I shown you my latest card trick?"

Melvin didn't have time for card tricks, but he did feel very tired. He kept his head down and peeked out the tree house window. If Carl got too close with that bologna, there'd be nothing Melvin could do. He scanned the sky for his partner in uncrime. Candace was his only hope now. But there was no sign of her, nothing in the sky but scattered clouds and—

Carl!

"Gotta go, Hugo," Melvin said as he headed out.

"Squeaker squeaken," said Hugo.

"What do you mean, you ate the last pretzel?" Melvin launched himself. Well, you know what happened.

Crash!

Splat!

Thud!

Kabonk!

It wasn't until he was up and flying

that he realized he'd understood what his rat had said. "How'd I do that?"

It didn't matter, because it never happened again. Melvin had just gotten lucky.

DOUBLE MEANWHILE . . .

"Country music, country music, country music." Candace kept up the chant as she flew across America. "Country music, country music, country music." She knew how her brain worked, especially while she was saving the world. In one ear, out the other. It was the same way with Melvin's math tutoring.

Eew . . . math.

Country music, country music, country music.

103

Candace was more of a rock-and-roll fan herself. Her favorite band was The Grateful Fred. She had all their CDs. And she played them loud to drown out her father's country music. Eew . . . country. She hated that stuff. Which, of course, is one of the main rules of childhood. Whatever your parents like, you shouldn't like, especially when it comes to music.

But right now she was glad for her father's music taste. This is another rule of childhood. Hate whatever your parents love, musically, but change your mind when it's to your advantage.

And right now Melvin needed help. Candace would have to borrow one of her father's CDs.

Country music, country music, country music.

Candace flew on and kept up the chant. So far her memory was working. No kicking in doors in Saint Louis this time. She flew directly home. When she got there she raced to the den where her father kept all his albums. It was a huge collection, shelf after shelf. He even had the Country Singer's Code tacked to the wall.

SINGER'S
CODE

Sing about your farm.
Sing about your truck.
When all else fails, sing about your dog.

You had to be serious about country music to have the Country Singer's Code on your wall. Candace grabbed one of the disks, then grabbed the portable CD player out of her room and some sandwich wrap from the kitchen. Sandwich wrap would protect her from the effects of the bologna if Carl got too close. She ran outside.

"Where are you, Melvin?" she said out loud. She stopped to listen. Nothing. No sign of her partner in uncrime.

CARL'S DEVIOUS AND SINISTER PLAN

It didn't take long for Carl to spot Melvin. He was the only other guy flying over Los Angeles without an airplane. The question was, could Carl catch him? True, Melvin couldn't get off the ground on the first try. But once he was up and flying he was as fast as the next superhero. And as long as he kept his distance, he would be unaffected by the bologna.

"Curses!" yelled Carl. This is what bad guys say when they're upset. Sometimes they say worse things—but not in this book. Whenever Carl sped up, Melvin did the same. When Carl zigged, Melvin zagged. When Carl went up, Melvin went down. The chase went on and on. All over Los Angeles. Up in the hills. Out to the beach. Between the tall buildings of downtown.

Carl looked at his supply of bologna. By the slab. By the slice. *Wait a minute,* he thought. *Those slices are round—like Frisbees.* Back at the academy, he had been great at throwing Frisbees. He reached into his bologna sack and grabbed a slice. Then, with a devious— or was it sinister?—grin, he licked it and flung it at Melvin.

It missed. But he kept on licking and flinging discs of lunch meat, rapid-fire.

Melvin dodged and weaved, looking back instead of forward. And that's why he didn't see the flagpole on the top of City Hall. *Clang!* He hit the pole doing 90. At the same moment, two slices hit him from behind. They stuck, thanks to Carl's spit. He may have been a bad guy, but he wasn't stupid.

"Gross, but effective," Carl said with a laugh.

Melvin was still seeing stars from hitting the pole. And now he was losing strength because of the bologna. He fell from the top of the building, bouncing off window ledges as he went. Down, down, down . . .

Splat!

And what a splat it was! Melvin staggered to his feet, the bologna still stuck to the back of his cape. Then he dropped to his knees, gasping, "Can't . . . move . . . get . . . me . . . out . . . of . . . here."

It was up to Candace now. She was his only hope.

Carl landed nearby and came toward Melvin. "Any last words?" he said as he grabbed Melvin by the throat.

"Candace."

"I said words, not word."

"Candace Brinkwater," Melvin said weakly.

CANDACE BRINKWATER'S
SUPER EARS

Candace launched herself from her front yard, holding her portable CD player and the sandwich wrap. She hovered to listen. Then she heard it. Someone was calling her name.

"Candace."

Then she heard it again.

"Candace Brinkwater."

It was Melvin!

She streaked through the sky. Then she heard something else.

"Can't . . . move . . . get . . . me . . . out . . . of . . . here."

Well, actually it was more like "Can't . . . aack . . . move . . . aack . . . get . . . aack . . . me . . ." You get the idea.

"Carl's monster choke hold!" Candace said. She zoomed back and forth between the tall buildings of downtown, searching. Then she heard it again.

"Can't . . . move . . . get . . . me . . . out . . . of . . . here."

Only this time it was "Aack . . . aack . . . aack . . . aack . . ."

And then she saw them, behind City Hall. Carl had Melvin in the hold, and Melvin was helpless. Candace dropped from the sky, being careful to keep her distance from the bologna. "Stop, in the name of the law!"

Melvin squeaked, "You mean, 'Not so fast.'" This was part of the Superhero's Code, of course, and Melvin always tried to teach Candace the code, even when he was having the life choked out of him.

"Whatever." Candace placed the CD player on the ground and pressed play. Nothing happened. *Holy no batteries!* she thought.

Holy no batteries, indeed! Better think of something quick, Candace. Your partner in uncrime is turning blue.

Carl squeezed harder. Melvin gasped.

"Think," Candace said to herself. "Think." Then it came to her. The code. Of course, the Country Singer's Code.

Sing about your farm.
Sing about your truck.
When all else fails, sing about your dog.

All else had failed. Melvin was at the mercy of Carl. Only Candace could save him now. She opened her mouth and began to sing, "I am a dog of constant sorrow . . ."

She sang and sang.

"I eat kibble all my days . . ."

"Holy lousy lyrics," said Carl. He still held on to Melvin, but his grip was starting to weaken.

"Holy lousy lyrics, indeed!" gasped Melvin as color returned to his face. "Keep singing, Candace!"

Candace did. She sang on and on.

"I sure hate that kibble. Throw me a burger and let me graze." She added some twang to her voice and every once in a while a *y'all* and *yee-ha*. *Y'all* and *yee-ha* were not part of the Country Singer's Code as far as she knew, but she had to extend the song for Melvin's sake.

Carl let go of Melvin's throat and staggered. He grabbed onto the building to keep from falling.

"Keep singing," yelled Melvin.

Candace sang and sang, all about the constant sorrow of losing her dog Smed. And the more she kept it up, the weaker Carl became. Then, without even thinking about it, she tossed in *yeah* and *baby* a few times. She was combining the Country Singer's Code with the Rock and Roller's Code. But it was working anyway.

Carl fell to his knees, gasping, "Can't . . . move . . . get . . . me . . . out . . . of . . . here."

Melvin grabbed the bologna from his cape and tossed it as far as his weak arms would allow. Then he removed Carl's cape and tossed that aside. Once he'd regained his strength, he grabbed Carl and carried him over to Candace.

"You saved my life, Candace," Melvin said. "How can I ever thank you?"

"Hey, you're my partner in uncrime. You'd do the same for me."

Melvin knew what the proper response was according to the Superhero's Code, but he liked Candace's reply better. They were teammates, partners in uncrime, and once again Los Angeles was a better place because of them.

They slapped a high-five. "Let's put this guy where he belongs," Melvin said.

Carl gritted his teeth. "I hate your guts, Melvin Beederman. And your little pal, too."

"Save it for the judge," Melvin told him.

THE JUDGE THROWS
THE BOOK AT CARL

Carl ducked, and the book hit a lawyer. "Ouch!" said the lawyer. It was a pretty big book.

"I sentence you to one year of service on the *Good Ship Lollipop*," the judge said. Since Carl was only a kid, he couldn't go to jail. But to be a bad guy on a ship called *Lollipop* was even worse.

"No, no, anything but that," yelled Carl. "I beg you, put me on a chain gang somewhere. Send me to prison."

"One year washing dishes on the *Good Ship Lollipop*," the judge said. He was a pretty strict judge, and he liked Candace and Melvin. "No one messes with our superheroes."

So Carl was sent away to begin his one-year sentence, and life in Los

Angeles returned to normal. Our two partners in uncrime went back to doing what they did best—working math problems and catching bad guys.

"Up, up, and away," Melvin said, the next day at the library.

Crash!

Splat!

Thud!

Kabonk!

"Some things never change," Candace said as they streaked across the sky.

Melvin looked down and saw the people of Los Angeles in their underwear. "I know what you mean." But for now he didn't care. He was just glad that he and Candace were still a team, and that he wouldn't have to worry about Carl for a very long time.

Meanwhile . . . in the middle of the Atlantic Ocean, Carl was in his room on the *Good Ship Lollipop*. He had just finished the evening dishes, and now he was alone without even a laptop computer to send Melvin a nasty e-mail. He looked through his porthole window.

"I have to get out of here," he said to himself. But how? There was nothing but water as far as the eye could see.

There had to be a way to escape. He began looking through the things in his sea chest. And then he saw it. Of course! The inflatable lair! Things that inflate also float. Carl waited until three in the morning, when all was quiet, then he hauled his lair up on deck. He pulled the self-inflating device, pushed the lair over the side, and jumped on.

"No more washing dishes for me," he said with a fiendish laugh. "Look out, Melvin Beederman. I'm going to get you, if it's the last thing I do!"

Carl floated away to freedom. He was in the middle of nowhere, which, as everyone knows, is right next to somewhere. And this gave him all the time in the world to come up with devious and sinister plans to get back at Melvin Beederman and his partner in uncrime. Someday he would be back. He was sure of it.

"Someday I'll be back," he said. "I'm sure of it."

He had no idea he wasn't supposed to repeat what the narrator says, but, hey, what do you expect from a bad guy?

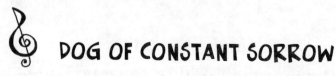

DOG OF CONSTANT SORROW

LYRICS BY CANDACE BRINKWATER

*(to the tune of "I Am a Man of Constant Sorrow,"
a traditional bluegrass song)*

I am a dog of constant sorrow,
I eat kibble all my days.
I sure hate that stinkin' kibble.
Throw me a burger and let me graze,
Throw me that burger, let me graze.

I love to chase that nervous mailman.
He doesn't like it, but that is tough.
I chew on shoes and dig up bones.
Oh, I just can't get enough.
Those yummy bones, can't get enough.

I like to scratch and pee on hydrants,
That is what I always do.
But the most fun that I have ever found
Is chasing cars and sniffing poo.
Yup, chasing cars and sniffing poo.

But these cars speed by so doggone fast,
They ran me over and I went splat.
I went splat, like Melvin Beederman,
But I am dead now and that is that.
I sure am dead, and that is that.

Now up in this ol' doggy heaven
I thought I'd dine on juicy steak.
But all they have is stinkin' kibble,
What constant sorrow and heartbreak!
Yup, constant sorrow and heartbreak.

WHO IS CARL?

Like all students at the Superhero Academy, Carl was an orphan. His parents were killed by an evil wizard, who then turned his wrath on Carl and—

Oops! Wrong story!

Carl lived with his father who was an auto mechanic. One day the Buick his father was working on fell off the jack and crushed him. Poor Carl wasn't able to save his father that day, but he has been bench-pressing Buicks ever since. He was sent to an orphanage, across town from where Melvin had been placed. The two boys met for the first time at the all-city kickball championships for orphaned children. And the rivalry began.

How can a kid with goofy hair run so fast? thought Carl.

Carl was later sent to the Superhero Academy, where he excelled in train-stopping, flying, and computer skills. The rivalry between him and Melvin continues to this day. He wants to get Melvin if it's the last thing he does.

SKETCHBOOK OF TERROR

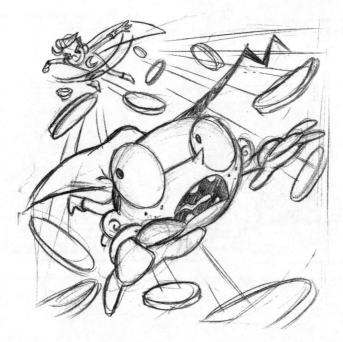

And now, a superheroic excerpt from

MELVIN BEEDERMAN SUPERHERO

BOOK 5

THE FAKE CAPE CAPER

Superhero Melvin Beederman was sitting on top of City Hall, taking a break. It had been a busy morning of catching bad guys, sinister sleazeballs, and devious dudes . . . not to mention devious dames. Twelve drug dealers, seven car thieves, two bank robbers, and one guy who was just *thinking* about taking over the world. He had that I'm-thinking-of-taking-over-the-world look on his face.

Melvin had seen that expression before, and he decided to put a stop to it before it got out of hand.

But now it was break time, or rather, lunch time, and Melvin sat eating pretzels and drinking root beer on top of one of the tallest buildings in Los Angeles. *This is my town,* he said to himself as he looked around. It was. Melvin was the superhero in charge of L.A. Along with his sidekick Candace Brinkwater, he  kept the peace and lunched on top of tall buildings as often as possible.

Suddenly one of the pretzels started ringing.

Melvin jumped. "Holy high-tech

snack food. I forgot all about my pretzel phone."

Holy high-tech snack food indeed! He had forgotten.

Melvin had purchased the pretzel phone at Sneaky Sam's Gadgets for Good Guys. As everyone knows, Sneaky Sam provided crime-fighting tools to California's secret agents and super-heroes since 1942.

The pretzel phone rang again and Melvin answered it. "Hello, Melvin Beederman here."

"Melvin! This is Superhero James."

"James!" Melvin was so excited he almost fell off the building. Almost. James had been one of Melvin's best friends back at the Superhero Academy.

"What's up? Catch any bad guys lately?"

"More than I can count."

"I know what you mean," Melvin said, although he always counted them.

"Listen, Melvin, I called to see if you are going to the Superhero Convention in Las Vegas."

"Superhero Convention? What about my day job? I'm in charge of Los Angeles, you know." Melvin took saving the world seriously.

"Put your sidekick in charge for a few days," James suggested. "That's what Margaret and I are doing."

Superhero Margaret was Melvin's other best friend from the Superhero Academy. Melvin hadn't seen either of them in months. Going to Las Vegas sounded great. That Superhero Convention sounded even better. And seeing his two best friends in the whole world sounded best of all.

"What do you say, Melvin buddy?"

Melvin wasn't sure if his sidekick, Candace Brinkwater, could handle the job. After all, she had not graduated from the academy. She was just the girl with whom he had decided to divide his cape, and this was all because of a mistake made at the dry cleaners. Could she handle Los Angeles all by herself? It was hard to say. What if Max the Wonder Thug went on a crime spree? Or Calamity Wayne, for that matter?

Still, he really wanted to see James and Margaret.

Melvin decided to go for it and hope for the best. "I'll be there," he said. "When is it?"

"It starts tomorrow and lasts all week. Didn't you get a flyer in the mail?"

"I live in a tree house, James. I don't exactly have an address."

This was true. Melvin lived in a tree house overlooking the city. From there he could spot crimes before they happened and occasionally catch guys who were just thinking about doing devious or sinister deeds—like taking over the world.

"See you in Vegas," James said.

"Yeah, see you there." Melvin hung up

the pretzel. He was still hungry and had a sudden urge to eat his phone. Instead he put it in his pocket so he wouldn't be tempted.